Wally's Magical Adventures

Adapted by Kristen L. Depken
Based on the episodes "Naptime for Borgelorp" by Adam Peltzman and "This Rock Can Talk" by Tim McKeon
Illustrated by Benjamin Burch

A GOLDEN BOOK • NEW YORK

© 2015 Viacom International Inc. All rights reserved. Published in the United States by Golden Books, an imprint of Random House Children's Books, a division of Random House LLC, 1745 Broadway, New York, NY 10019, and in Canada by Random House of Canada Limited, Toronto, Penguin Random House Companies. Golden Books, A Golden Book, A Big Golden Book, the G colophon, and the distinctive gold spine are registered trademarks of Random House LLC. Nickelodeon, Wallykazam!, and all related titles, logos, and characters are trademarks of Viacom International Inc.
randomhousekids.com
ISBN 978-0-385-38766-8
Printed in the United States of America
10 9 8 7 6 5 4 3 2 1

Naptime for Borgelorp

All the magic words in this story start with the letter **s**.

One day, Wally Trollman and his pet dragon, Norville, went to visit their friend Ogre Doug.

Ogre Doug needed someone to babysit one of his pets, a borgelorp named Borgelorp.

"I have to go to the store to buy food for my pet mammoth, and Borgelorp is just too little to leave alone," said Ogre Doug.

"Aww," said Wally when he saw the adorable little creature. "We'll look after him!"

"Great! All you have to do is get him to take a nap," said Ogre Doug. "And one more thing. Whatever you do, do not let him eat any purple flowers."

"No purple flowers," Wally said to Norville. "We'd better remember that."

Wally picked up Borgelorp. "Okay, time for your nap," he said.

"No nap. . . . Play!" shouted Borgelorp. He jumped out of Wally's hands and onto his head. "Play! Play! Play!" Then he ran off.

Wally had an idea. "We'll use my magic stick to make something Borgelorp can play with . . . and get him *really* tired. Hmm. All the magic words start with the **s** sound today. So how about . . . a **sock**?"

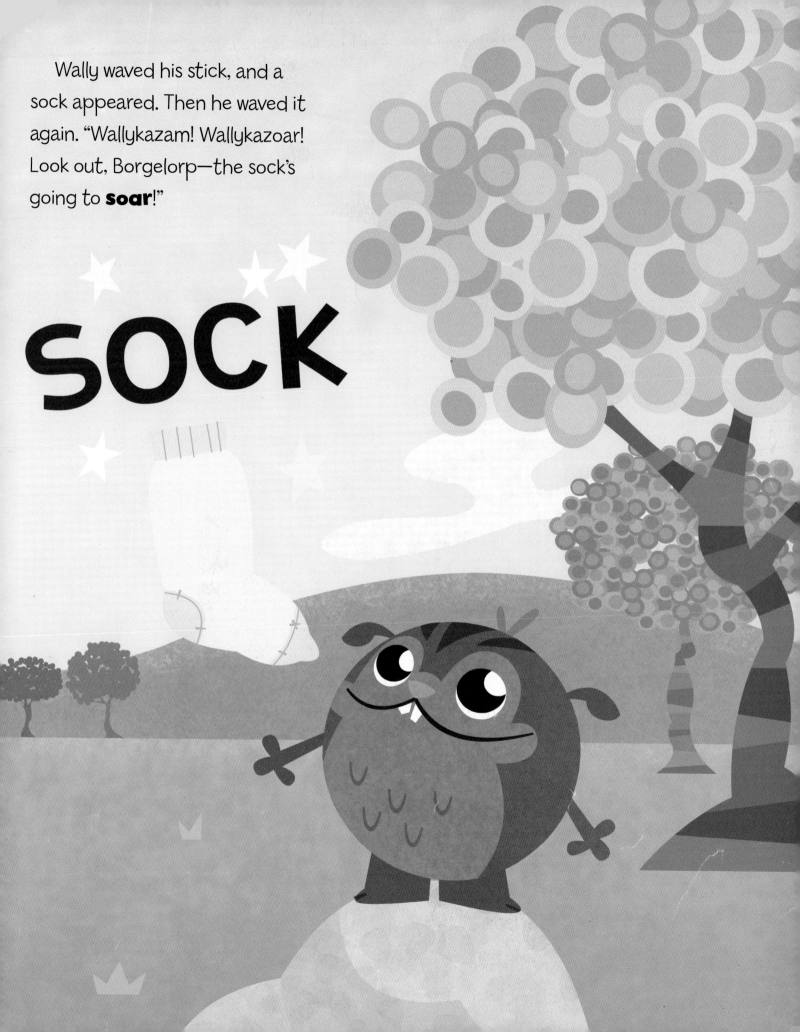

Wally waved his stick, and a sock appeared. Then he waved it again. "Wallykazam! Wallykazoar! Look out, Borgelorp—the sock's going to **soar**!"

SOCK

Borgelorp chased the sock . . . right into a field of purple flowers!
Wally gasped. "What if he eats one? I'd better give him something
else to eat."

He waved his magic stick, and a **sandwich** appeared. Borgelorp
chomped on it happily.

Just then, Bobgoblin popped out of his house.

"Wally Trollman, why can't he eat a purple flower?"

"We don't know, but Ogre Doug said it's not allowed," replied Wally.

"But Bobgoblin wants to give him a purple flower!" said Bobgoblin, holding one out to Borgelorp.

Wally scooped up Borgelorp and walked away.

Bobgoblin crossed his arms. "Bobgoblin WILL give him a purple flower!"

Wally and Norville took Borgelorp to visit their friend Gina Giant.

"I know how to get Borgelorp to nap!" said Gina. She prepared a comfy bed for him. Then she had Wally use his magic stick to make a **soft song**.

It was working! Borgelorp was almost asleep, when suddenly— "Purple flower!" Bobgoblin appeared out of nowhere and gave Borgelorp a purple flower! *Chomp!*

Pop! Borgelorp turned purple!
Before Wally could stop him, Bobgoblin
tossed him another purple flower. *Whoosh!*

"Purple flowerrrrrs!" Borgelorp shouted,
and took off running. Wally, Gina, Norville,
and Bobgoblin chased him. He was heading
to Purple Flower Mountain!

"We have to stop him!" cried Wally.

Wally and his friends reached the top of Purple Flower Mountain in time to see Borgelorp eating every purple flower he could. Suddenly, Borgelorp began to grow . . .

. . . and grow . . .

. . . and grow.

Soon he was enormous! He slid down the mountain and started running toward town.
Wally waved his magic stick. **"Stop!"** he called.
But the magic word missed Borgelorp and stopped Bobgoblin instead.

The giant Borgelorp ran through town and stomped past Bobgoblin's house.
"Hey!" said Bobgoblin. "This must stop!"
Wally had a plan. "Bobgoblin, can you get Borgelorp to chase you?"

Bobgoblin waved some purple flowers
in front of Borgelorp, who began to chase
him in circles.

While Borgelorp was busy, Wally and Gina Giant prepared
a place for him to nap.

"And now for a **soft song**," said Wally with a wave of his stick.
But the song was too soft for the giant Borgelorp to hear.

"I know an **s** word that can help!" said Gina. "**Symphony!** It's music with lots and lots of instruments, so everyone can hear it."
Wally waved his stick, and a symphony began to play.
Soon Borgelorp was fast asleep!

"Can you believe it?" asked Wally. "We finally got Borgelorp to nap!" But his friends were asleep, too!

A few minutes later, Ogre Doug arrived.

"Oh, good—Borgelorp is napping!" he said.

"He also ate some purple flowers," said Wally. "Sorry. We tried to stop him."

"That's okay, Wally," said Ogre Doug with a shrug. "You just have to do this."

He reached over and pressed the sleeping Borgelorp's nose.

Boop! Borgelorp shrank back to his normal size.

"*Now* he tells us," said Wally, and he and Ogre Doug shared a laugh while their friends—especially Borgelorp—enjoyed their naps.

The Really, Really, Really Big Treasure

All the magic words in this story start with the letter **t**.

One day, Wally and Norville were in the forest, playing with a tuba. Bobgoblin grabbed the tuba, took a deep breath, and blew as hard as he could.

The noise was so loud, the ground started to shake! All the shaking caused a rock to roll down a nearby mountain. It landed right next to Wally and Norville.

"Told you Bobgoblin was the loudest," said Bobgoblin. He asked if he could keep the tuba, but Wally barely noticed—he was too busy looking at the rock.

"I wonder where this rock came from," said Wally. "Too bad rocks can't talk."

Then Wally remembered that the day's magic letter was **t**. He waved his magic stick and said, "Wallykazam! Wallykazalk! Let's hear this big rock **talk**!"

"How's it going?" said the rock. "I'm Rockelle. I've been dying to tell somebody about the really, really, really big treasure."

Wally gasped. Everyone had heard of the really, really, really big treasure, but no one knew where it was.

"It's buried at the top of the mountain, where I live," Rockelle said.

"We can go on a treasure hunt and dig it up!" said Wally.

There was one problem: Rockelle couldn't walk!
"Just roll me," she told Wally and Norville.
They rolled Rockelle past a tree where
Bobgoblin was playing his tuba. When
Bobgoblin heard they were going
to look for the really, really, really big
treasure, his ears pricked up.
He hugged his tuba close and
whispered, "We can sneak past them,
Tuba, and get to the treasure before
Wally!" He raced after his friends.

Things were rolling along smoothly until Wally, Norville, and Rockelle reached a river. How would they get Rockelle across without sinking?

Wally pulled out his magic stick. "We just need something Rockelle can float on," he said. "Like a . . . **tube**!"

A giant rubber tube appeared under Rockelle, and they floated safely across the river.

toboggan

Soon the three friends reached the bottom of the mountain path.

"Let's climb that mountain!" said Wally. He and Norville tried to roll Rockelle up the path, but she was too heavy.

"Maybe we can put you on something," suggested Wally.

"A **t** word, right?" asked Rockelle. "How about a toboggan? It's a big sled."

Wally flicked his magic stick, and a **toboggan** appeared.

"Hmm. We could use something to help the toboggan go faster," said Wally. He waved his stick again. **"Tires!"**

Once the toboggan had tires, they were on their way to the treasure!

Just then, Bobgoblin appeared.

"What are you doing here?" asked Wally.

"Trying to get the treasure," said Bobgoblin. "I mean—nothing." With that, Bobgoblin started running up the path.

"We've got to get there first!" said Wally. They tried to follow Bobgoblin. When they reached a fallen tree that was blocking the path, Bobgoblin climbed to the other side, but Wally and Norville couldn't get Rockelle over it.

Wally took out his magic stick. "We need a hole—
or a **tunnel**!" he said.

A tunnel opened in the tree, and Wally and his
friends hurried through it.

They reached a rope bridge. They tried to cross it, but Rockelle was too heavy. The bridge broke! They were falling into a deep ravine.

"We need something soft to land on," said Wally. "How about . . . **taffy**?"
He waved his magic stick, and they landed safely on a big, gooey pile of taffy.

They were safe, but they were also far from the top of the mountain.
Luckily, Wally thought of another **t** word. **"Top!"** he cried.

Poof! Wally, Norville, and Rockelle were instantly at the top of the mountain.

Rockelle showed Wally and Norville where the treasure was buried, and Norville started digging.

"I can see the really, really, really big treasure!" said Wally.

But just as they pulled it out of the ground, Bobgoblin appeared. He leapt on top of the treasure chest and rode it down the mountain!

"We need to get down this mountain fast!" cried Wally. He took out his magic stick and used three **t** words to help them.

They **tumbled**.

They **turned**.

And they bounced across the river on a **trampoline**!

They caught up to Bobgoblin at the bottom of the mountain.
"Bobgoblin, you didn't find this treasure chest—we did!" said Wally.
"So we get to see what's inside."
They opened the treasure chest and saw a tiny box at the bottom.

"That's the really, really, really big treasure?" asked Wally.

"Sorry I took you guys on that big trip just for that little thing," said Rockelle.

"I had a great time! Plus we met you," said Wally. He picked up the tiny box. "Might as well see what's inside."

He opened the little box . . .

. . . and a giant golden bouncy castle popped out!

"It *is* a really, really, really big treasure!" said Wally.

Wally, Bobgoblin, and Norville all jumped into the castle. But Rockelle couldn't jump.

Wally had an idea. He waved his magic stick. **"Toss!"** he shouted, and Rockelle was magically tossed into the castle.

Everyone spent the rest of the day bouncing in the castle— even Bobgoblin and his beloved tuba.